For Cosima, with love

Sea life

In the deep blue sea, somewhere
between Europe and Africa,
there live many animals: Lots of
colourful fish and crabs. They swim
around happily, talk to each other
and play funny games together.

GARBAGE I

In the middle of a warm mid-summer day, a man in a boat comes and throws rubbish into the water: glass bottles, tins and plastic bags. "Hey, what's that?" says Polly, a nice red fish. "What is the man doing? Is he crazy?!"

GARBAGE I

Some days later the man in the boat comes again. This time he has got canisters and he pours oil into the water. He also throws part of an old bike into the water.
"We must do something," says Lucy, a fish girl with wonderful orange and yellow stripes. "Let's meet this afternoon at two o'clock."

PROTEST

Lots of animals come to the meeting. "Swimming around isn't fun anymore," says Pinky, a pink cuttlefish. "The water is dirty and there's oil everywhere!"
Jimmy, a yellow starfish and Julie, a little crab, are very angry:
"I've hurt my finger on the glass bottles!" Julie cries.

PROTEST

"I've got an idea," says Billy. Billy is a shark. "Next time the man comes, I'll jump out of the water and show him my teeth. And then he'll never come back!"

GARBAGE I

On the next day the man in the boat comes back again. His boat is full of rubbish. But this time he isn't alone. A little boy is in the boat, too. He leans forward and – with a big splash – falls into the water.

danger
help
help

Two little seahorses watch everything and cry: "Help! The little boy needs help!" Two dolphins come along. "Please, help the boy!" the seahorses say.

GARBAGE

Billy and the two dolphins pull the boy out of the water and bring him back to the boat. "Thank you very much!" the man says to the animals. The dolphins and the shark don't answer.

GARBAGE I

The boy's clothes are full of oil and
a plastic bag is sticking to his body.
"I told you it's not right to throw
all these things into the ocean!"
the little boy says to his father.
"The animals saved my life!"

GARBAGE I CLEAN SEA I